Glasses, Wallet, Keys

STORIES

JOHN COLLINS WILLIAMS

.

Glasses, Wallet, Keys

Stories

John Collins Williams

ISBN (Print Edition): 978-1-66788-091-4

ISBN (eBook Edition): 978-1-66788-092-1

To Stephanie, always.

CONTENTS

GLASSES, WALLET, KEYS

What the fuck? Shit everywhere! Drips, streaks, plops. Jackson Pollocked the carpet. Stinking up the whole downstairs. She looks back at me: brown eyes, no pupils, face of shame. It's my fault. Slept in. Can't be mad at her. She curls up on her bed, nose down. Poor thing; fourteen years old and no longer in control. This will take time. And a lot of paper towels. Sponges, Nature's Miracle, vat of Febreze. Search the cabinets. Out of everything. *Fuck!* No choice. Haven't been out in a week.

Shower. Brush. Dress.

Pat my temple, my butt, my pocket: glasses, wallet, keys. Where are the goddamn car keys? Counter? Other counter? Nope. She left her jacket. Shake it. Thank God! Grab the shopping bags: save the planet. Gloves. Coat. Hat. Scarf. Phone. Head to the car. Beep the door and climb in. Press Here. Lights and chimes. Every machine sings.

See my breath.

Think.

Keys. Wallet. Bags. Mask.

Fuck! Mask!

Search the car. Door pocket. Glove compartment. Floor. Floor. Under the seat. Old one. Her lipstick. Gross.

Short drive. Paper towels, sponges. What else? Something for lunch and dinner? Can't think about food with a house full of shit. List: Corgi. Cats. Kibble. Cans. Paper towels will be a problem. Paper anything. Napkins. Garbage bags. *I'm starving.* Carpet cleaner. A pickup truck passes me with a torn American flag waving behind. Another bumper in front: Blue Lives Matter. Signaling to each other. I am surrounded. We are masked. We are unmasked.

Stop & Shop. Short line out front. Social distance. Grim faces. Mask up, eyes down. Smell her. Wipe down the cart. Arrows on the floor, one-way traffic. Eyes feel assaulted. Make it quick. Wrong way to cleaning products. Scan the shelves. Follow the list. Lysol. Paper towels! I'm in luck. Line to pay. Takes forever. Breath fogs my glasses. Escape!

Carry corgi into the yard. Followed by the rug: a goner. Get to work. On hands and knees, spray bottle. Towel up the poop, plop by streak. One little dog! Crack open the windows. Febreze the house. Take the garbage bag out to the garage. Where is she? Search the yard. Call her name.

Trot to the back. Nope. Run to the front. Scan the street. *Fuck!* Freezing. Run back in. Jacket, glasses, wallet, keys. Leash! Still have some poop on my fingers.

No need to panic. Happens all the time. Neighbors will bring her back. "Is she yours?" Little rascal! Walk the block, scanning low. Call her name.

Jingle the leash: her favorite sound. Second favorite sound: should have brought some kibble. Turn the corner. Check Main Street. Imagine a guttered lump of fur and blood. Nothing. Circumnavigate the block. Forgot my mask. Back to the house. Check the yard again.

Empty.

Stop.

Think.

Feel her absence. Corgi here. Corgi gone.

Breathe.

Up the street again to the dock and back. Searching, calling, jingling. Remember the time I went looking for her and found her following me. *No problem here, officer!* Turn around to check. Starting to feel my heartbeat. Go back and wash my hands. Could she have gotten inside? Impossible. Circle the downstairs. Run up and check: hallway, bathroom, boy's room, bedroom. Corgi. Son. Wife.

Sit on the top step and listen to the empty house. Distant traffic. Gulls. Tinnitus. Breaths. I had looked forward to this: solitude.

Last week was great. Refrigerator full of food. Watched Antonioni movies all day and fell in love with Monica Vitti. Oh, my God, Monica Vitti! *Che faccia!* Like, back in college with Louise Brooks. I could look at her for hours. She was alive to me. Though dead. As is Monica. Gorgeous, though. *Misteriosa.* Slept in. Fed the corgi and the cats. Small meals. Filmed entertainment. Quiet. Peace. Me time.

Last night, she called: boy doesn't want to leave school. OK in the dorm, taking classes online. Better than home with us.

"Told you," I said.

"You did not."

OK, not technically. Big fight before she left.

"You're babying him," I said. "We can't rescue him every time."

"It's a fucking pandemic," she said. "You're cold. I don't know you," she said.

Off she went. Six-hour drive.

Now:

"I'm staying."

"For how long?"

She didn't answer. Airbnb.

And a thought, deep thought, dark thought, forbidden thought, began to form: *Is this how it happens?*

"It's nice up here," she said.

Hung up and waited for a feeling.

Thought: *Ciao, Monica!*

It occurs to me: last time she went missing, really missing—flyers-on-telephone-poles and lost-pet-Facebook-group missing—I found her at the vet around the corner. So, I call.

"Has anyone brought in a missing corgi?"

"Boy or girl?"

"Girl."

"With diarrhea?"

Glasses, wallet, keys, mask, leash. When they bring her out, she seems to barely recognize me. Nonchalant.

The nurse says, "Corgis are so adorable!"

"That's how they get you," I say.

Make an appointment for tomorrow.

Dream of Larchmont. Murray Avenue School. Lookout Circle. Kerry Dancer. The Duck Pond. Childhood. The streets do not match my memory. Wake up wondering, *Where is the Duck Pond? Off Chatsworth?* Images clear but don't connect. Maybe I could take a drive . . . then, I sniff. Rise with dread. Downstairs: *Shit Show, Part Two*. Not as bad. But still. Another rug ruined. She looks at me again; *so adorable!* Paper towels, hands and knees, Nature's Miracle. Poor thing.

Glasses, watch, wallet, keys, phone, mask, leash, car, corgi. Vet is Russian. Heavy accent. Catch every third word. Corgi on table scale, growls. Hold her head, stroke her ears. She's pissed at me. Losing weight. Could be a lot of things: UTI, liver, kidneys, cancer. Bottom line: two antibiotics, probiotics, stool sample, blood work. Seven hundred dollars. We both leave miserable.

Together on the couch. Stroke her head. Can't concentrate on filmed entertainment. Can't read. Think about the Duck Pond. Chemical smells. Nauseous. She repositions her butt toward me: *Scratch there. No! There!* Impatient. Brown eyes. Red-tan coat. Thick white chest. Widow's peak. Fairy Saddle. Love this dog. Every hour, carry her to the yard. She makes it through the night. Gobbles her kibble and pills. She's loving this. *Asshole.*

Next day, vet calls. "Blood work mixed. Could be cancer. Need to do imaging."

"What about her pain?"

He levels with me. "Some dogs live to sixteen, some eighteen. Yours won't. You have maybe a year with her. She's passed her expiration date."

Sit on the floor and hold her. She growls. Don't care. Kiss her ears and head. Squeeze my expired corgi. "Who's my girl? Who's my girly girl? " She snarls. This little dog. The boy was four. I was forty.

"Midlife Crisis Corgi," she declared.

How did she get old? How did I? Choke up. She yelps and squirms free. Shakes her floppy ears. Looks at me. Searches my face. Yawns.

Kerry Dancer didn't growl when you held her. Picture my father sitting on the porch steps, petting her. Mom standing over him.

"My life is shit," he sobbed.

I watched the back of them through the door glass. Scared. Never seen him cry. She came inside. He sat for a while, glanced back at me, lost, and then drove home, drunk.

Corgi beside me in bed, breathing. Can't sleep. Nuzzle her head. Favorite smells: corgi ear, baby head, nape of neck. Never smell baby head again. Eighteen. Squirms when I hug him. Pats me on the head. And her neck? Next to me every night . . .

Make a list. Glasses, wallet, keys. Phone, computer, charger. House, car, job. Money, sex. Mother, brother, sister. Health. Breath. Food. Water. Sleep. Books. Film. Dreams. Memory. Longing. Desire. Clothes. Watch. Masks. Habits. Roles. Duties. Debts.

Love.

Marriage.

Son.

Dream of the Duck Pond again. Frozen. Skates with double blades: I'm four or five. Dad and Mom. Brother and baby sister. Before the corgis. Before divorce. *Family.*

She barks me up. Carry her out to pee. Her legs shake. I shiver.

Kibble, canned food, pills, and powder: she laps it up.

Out again. She assumes the position: solid dump. So proud of her.

Feelings I can name: pride, exhaustion, anxiety, loneliness, longing, tenderness.

Carry her in. Listen to the house. Emptiness. Sadness. Shame.

Love is a verb.

Text the cat sitter. No reply. *Fuck!*

Suitcase: pants, shirts, sweaters, socks, underwear, toothbrush, toothpaste, razors, shaving cream. Advil, Lexapro.

Text again.

Headphones, boots, computer, iPad, charger, other charger, notebook.

Lug it downstairs.

Text again.

Kibble, cans, pills, powders, bowl, leash, dog bed.

Text again.

Fill the cats' bowl. Water. Cat box! Forgot about their shit entirely. Big job. *My life is shit!* Almost funny.

Litter. Camera. Film.

D*ing!* She can do it. Cats will live. Venmo.

Pack the car. Carry the corgi to the passenger seat.

Ignition. Chimes and lights. Plug in the phone. Six hours. Seatbelt. Gas.

Breathe.

Think.

Glasses. Wallet. Keys. Masks. Bag. Gloves. Coat. Hat. Scarf. Computer. Charger. Corgi. Kibble. Cans. Leash. Bowl. Pills. Powders. Paper towels. Febreze. Son. Wife.

She sits up and shakes her head. Looks at me, as if to say: go.

Go!

UNCLE DUCK

Richard (Dick, Uncle Duck, The Duck) Flannigan could not pass his upstairs bathroom without stopping to look. Sometimes he'd go in, whether he needed to or not, to just sit and admire: the clean white tiles, the shiny new tub, the chrome of the faucets. The comforting silence of the house. Sometimes, though, it made him uneasy. How Billy built this. How Billy left.

When his nephew tore out the old bathroom, however, it was the opposite of comforting. Dick winced at every crack and crumble as the old john was torn out and tossed into a pile in the backyard. Something so permanent, so familiar, ripped to shreds and ejected so scornfully: the shower, the old tub with the claw-and-ball feet, the toilet that fit him so comfortably, upturned and shattered.

Billy just said one morning, a few days after his arrival, his hair wet from the shower, "Uncle Duck, I'm going to fix up your bathroom."

"Why?"

"Because it's old."

"What's wrong with that?"

"You're my uncle, and I owe you one."

Billy didn't owe him anything. After all he'd been through (*Prison! Drugs! Don't tell me!*), Dick was glad to have him. Someone to do the dishes was more than what he was hoping for. Or play music with again. *But this*... The house, a rough-hewn, renovated barn at the edge of a cornfield, shuddered with every blow. Solstice, his cat and dearest companion, had taken off into the bushes that morning and would not come when called. Dick couldn't take it.

The old Volvo shuddered into ignition, and the joyous swing of a Bix Beiderbecke tape filled the car. Dick turned left toward town. *This isn't right. Billy shouldn't be doing this. But it's too late. The guts torn out. How long is he planning to stay anyway?* They had never discussed it exactly. Looking to the right, Dick saw Pete's house and the deep, man-made pond on the property ... a thin tan body, flat on the small dock above it. *Is it her?*

Approaching town, Dick wondered if there was anything he needed. Food? No, Billy had just gone shopping. Hardware? Billy had too much of that. He slowed down as he passed the church and turned right. Lunch? He wasn't hungry. He didn't want to deal with people. He'd been getting looks in town ever since his ex-con nephew moved in. He was sure of it. *Enough of people.* He drove past the town and was soon heading back to the main road. He paused at the stop sign and idled. *Which way?* A pickup pulled up behind him and the big grill filled his rearview. Dick signaled and turned left, toward the lake. *Just sit for a while. Can't go back just yet.*

Billy was his sister Mary's eldest, the most difficult of that troubled brood of five children. Dick was twenty-six when he first held the baby, his first nephew. He knew, even as he cradled (briefly, it made him too nervous) that squirmy warm ball of pink skin, that he would know unclehood but never fatherhood. Tall and awkward, prone to crushes, his brief forays into actual relationships with women had been disasters. Instead, he chose the banjo—for family, Mary's kids. He vowed to know this boy and be part of his life. But Dick was already living upstate, playing and teaching music, too far away for anything but the occasional telephone report and increasingly crowded annual visits. He became Uncle Dick and then Uncle Duck. He hated the nickname coined by Billy's sister Shannon. It was just a play on sounds: Dick, Duck. Kids aren't always charming. Anyway, Duck stuck. As for Billy, he became the charmer who was always in trouble, his fortunes forever rising and falling, the focus of the family's worry. Billy had visited for a few weeks one summer vacation, when he was about sixteen, and had discovered a natural ability on the guitar. He and Dick bonded—perhaps more than with any of his other nieces and nephews—and then he was gone. By the time Billy ended up in jail (at the same age Dick was when he first held him), nephew and uncle had been strangers for years.

Cars were parked along both shoulders of the road, leading to the lake. *People!* Dick turned around and headed back toward home. *Her tan body.* What would be his reason to stop by? What would he say? But as he approached her property, the dread of his own invaded house was enough to turn his wheels up her long gravel driveway. The old car rattled to a halt outside her kitchen, the immaculate kitchen of her perfectly restored house. He felt large and lumbering as he approached the brick walk to her door. She was standing behind the screen, smiling. She was wearing a denim shirt over her bathing suit.

"Howdy, you!"

"Hey, Pete. Have you seen Solstice?"

"Is he missing?" She opened the door for him, and he entered.

"He's not crazy about Billy. I haven't seen him all morning."

"So, this is a missing-cat visit? Not a social visit? Should we post flyers?"

Richard looked down at the tile floor and shook his head.

"Aw, not yet."

"I was making some tuna. Do you want some?"

She turned to the counter and opened a can. *She's a handsome woman,* he thought. Her skin was leathery brown and her dirty blonde hair was pulled back into a jumble. She was his age or thereabouts. A widow. She restored old houses and had a reputation for the exacting quality of her work. Her name was Anne, but people called her Pete. He didn't know why. And she liked him. Again, he didn't know why. But after nearly two years of friendship, the charge he felt in her presence still embarrassed him—disoriented him.

"Does he hate him?" Her voice was husky, direct like a man's.

Dick sat at the table. "He's not crazy about him. He shows up for his cans but then disappears. I see him watching me."

"Trust cats. They know."

"Billy's all right. He's fixing my bathroom. Gutting it completely."

"Really? An honest trade?" The singsong gave it away. She didn't like Billy; hated him on sight.

Dick thought he should defend him, but all he could come up with was, "He's full of surprises, I guess. I don't know him anymore."

"Poor Solstice."

"Hmnf."

The sandwiches were beautiful: fresh green lettuce, juicy garden tomatoes, whole-grain bread, a pickle. It was heaven in his mouth. They ate in silence on her deck under the umbrella. Dick relaxed. For the first time in days, he could hear the rustle of leaves and the buzz of the cicadas. He started to hear music in his head, the tune "I'll Get By" and the Billie Holiday recording, where she took those first three words and changed the intervals from thirds to three single notes and filled them with emotion. Satchmo did the same thing with "Stardust," singing one note in the first four measures. *Swing is rhythm.*

"Richard, we have to talk."

Bye-bye, Satchmo.

She smiled. "Look at your face!"

"What's wrong with my face?"

"Nothing; you have a lovely face. I just said, we have to talk."

Uh, oh. The worst four words in the English language. Dick had endured four actual relationships in his fifty-two years, and they had all ended with the same words.

"Is there something wrong?" he asked.

"Yes."

He felt his face flush and his pulse race.

"Richard, I'm glad you're coming around. I like being with you," she said. "But it's time we move this thing forward. It's time." She leaned forward. "It's time for you to ask me on a date."

Dick looked down at his half-eaten sandwich. His appetite was gone. She watched him. He felt nothing that he could name or describe. He just stared at his plate and waited for something, anything to say.

"Richard?"

"Yes?"

"Did you hear me?"

"Hmnf."

"What are you thinking?"

The second-worst four words. He concentrated. *The same note in a string of emotion.* The half-eaten sandwich. He still had no answer. Pete's hand grabbed his plate, and she disappeared into the house. He watched her moving in the darkness of the kitchen and heard the clatter of dishes on the counter.

"Pete!"

He picked up their glasses and walked into the kitchen. Her back was turned to him as she rinsed the dishes. He placed the glasses on the counter.

"Pete," he said softly.

"I have friends, you know. I don't need another *gentleman* friend." She placed the plates in the dishwasher. "Are you up to it or not, Richard?"

She faced him. He looked down.

"Sure."

"Are you going to ask me out? A proper date?"

"Sure, Pete."

"When?"

He sighed. Another feeling was rising in him: annoyance.

"When I'm ready. Geez!"

"Geez, Louise," she shot back. Then she smiled, and it was like a soft net breaking his fall but leaving him winded.

Billy was sitting on the kitchen stoop when Dick got back, drinking a beer beside the pile of debris that had been in his upstairs bathroom this morning. He was in worn jeans, shirtless, his torso muscular and sweaty, and he had a blurry tattoo on his left arm.

"Whatcha get?" Billy called, as his uncle stepped out of the Volvo. Dick just shrugged. His head was buzzing. He didn't want to be expected to say anything or be anything to anyone.

"Where'dja go?"

Dick paused, surveying the mess.

"And good riddance!" Billy said, nodding at the pile. "Mildew and mold under mildew and mold. You had a leak under the tub, did you know that? The floor was rotted through. One day, you would have climbed into the upstairs shower and be downstairs before you got out!"

Billy had a huge, aggressive smile. His square jaw and thick nose reminded Dick of his father, of himself.

"Say, Billy, how long is this going to take?"

"The bathroom?"

"Hmnf."

"Couple of days."

Dick scratched his head.

"I have students tomorrow."

"When?"

"All day. Starting at ten."

Billy tipped his beer bottle and drained it. He let out a big sigh.

"I dunno what to tell ya, Duck. It's gonna be a little awkward, I guess."

"Hmnf."

Dick looked away and saw a blur of black fur scurrying along the perimeter of his property.

It took more than a couple of days, and it was more than awkward. For a week, Dick taught banjo and guitar, sitting with his students on folding chairs in the yard, as the house shook and clattered in counter-rhythms behind them. Billy seemed to have saved his screaming power tools for the piano students. It was impossible.

One morning, Billy called out to him.

"Uncle Duck! Let me show you something."

Dick had avoided looking into the gutted bathroom, and now he knew why. Stripped to the studs, the tiny room was dark and barren. He could hardly picture what it used to look like. Billy was kneeling where the bathtub used to be. The old floor was replaced by fresh plywood. He had an open box in front of him.

"We need to decide what kind of shower faucet you want."

He held up a chrome disk.

"Instead of separate taps, we'll have one of these. Much more efficient."

Dick leaned in. He had no idea what he was looking at.

"I got a couple of options," Billy continued. "One's kinda rustic. This Old House and all. But I like the bright silver of this one, don't you?"

"Hmnf."

Billy looked up at him and then stood up to take in the room.

"I know it's hard to imagine."

Dick watched Billy shake his head softly and grin, as if he was looking at something completely different.

"It's gonna be fucking beautiful, Duck. I promise." He looked back at him. "So, chrome, right?"

Dick nodded grimly and turned away. What followed were days of sponge baths and careful avoidance. He took his meals when Billy was out at the hardware store. He hurried past the bathroom-in-progress, without looking in. He walked his property in the evenings to find Solstice, who would approach warily for his meals, all white face and cold eyes.

Of course, he had Pete on his mind as well. He tried to chase her ultimatum from his thoughts, but it was as insistent as Billy's hammering. Her friendship—a rare, late-in-life connection with a woman he truly admired—had come to mean comfort and companionship. She was easy to be with. He had naturally fantasized about more and had seen in her eyes what felt like an invitation once or twice. But given his history with women . . . she had no idea how bad he was at this stuff. A date was just the first step to disaster. And back to loneliness.

Dick played two gigs with the Skaneateles Dixieland Jazz Band the following week, strumming his frustration into his banjo. On Sunday, he broke two strings in the middle of the "Black Bottom Stomp." He came home that night to an empty house and a message scribbled almost illegibly on the kitchen pad: *Pete called. A woman? Call her ASAP.*

He climbed into bed but could not sleep. He was feeling guilty and cornered. *What to do?* He got up, put on his robe, and went to the living room. He took his banjo out of its case, sat on his La-Z-Boy, and began to pick a bluegrass pattern. The truth was, in spite of a lifetime's passion, he was not a natural musician. Music was a language that he had learned to speak after many years and lonely effort. This was not something a layman would hear—he was technically proficient and could play many instruments and styles—but he knew his limitations. Sometimes, when he played, it was like climbing a mountain with a summit that kept receding the harder he labored. But at other times, music entered the room like an old friend, and he felt like a listener more than a player, a witness bathed in warm vibrations. It was effortless tonight, a comfort, and he went with it. He took the bluegrass pattern through some jazz changes, and the two rivers collided and resolved themselves under his fingertips.

He closed his eyes and soon felt a soft warm body brush up against his leg. He looked down at the erect black tail and white face of Solstice. He stopped playing and stroked his friend's flat head and felt the purr through his fingertips.

"Hey, there, fella. How's my boy?"

Solstice flopped on his side and demanded a full-body rub. Dick leaned forward and obliged. The purring grew louder. The two of them were so caught up in their reunion that they didn't hear Billy's truck pull up. But Solstice cocked his ears at the sound of the car-door slam. When Billy pushed through the kitchen door, Solstice jumped up and ran.

"Oh, fella, where you goin'?" Dick called after him.

Dick heard the refrigerator door open and shut, followed by the sound of a beer bottle spitting open. Billy strode heavily into the living room and fell back into the couch and took a swig. "You're up!" he shouted.

"I was just going to bed." Dick leaned forward to place the banjo in its case.

"No! Play something for me. I haven't heard you really jam in, like, nine billion years."

"Oh, Billy, I've been playing all night. My fingers are sore."

"Are you pissed at me or something?"

Dick looked up at his nephew's glassy blue eyes. They seemed to search him. He lifted the banjo on to his lap and tuned up.

"Do you still play any of the things I taught you?"

"I used to. I was getting pretty good there. But you know, I haven't seen a guitar in a few fucking years."

Billy's face grew sullen. Dick started back into the bluegrass pattern, and Billy began to nod in rhythm, till a smile broke out wide on his face.

"Yeah, that's it." He took another drink.

Dick picked up the rhythm and Billy jumped up and started swaying his shoulders and dancing around the room. His movements were exaggerated with alcohol, and Dick watched him as he played, fearing that Billy would tumble over. He shifted to a slower rhythm, but Billy shook his head and called out, "No! No! Keep it up!" Dick obliged. Billy started jumping up and down. "That's it! Yeah!"

Dick watched him with alarm as Billy swallowed the last of his beer and danced, out through the kitchen and into the night, and began to howl at the top of his lungs.

"HEEEEYOOOWWWW!!"

Dick heard the beer bottle shatter against the porcelain. He stopped playing, put the banjo back in its case, and crossed to the kitchen. Through the screen door, he could see his nephew dancing and jumping in a circle around the pile of demolished bathroom, hooting and shouting in the night like a deranged shaman around an unlit bonfire.

"That's right! Fuck YOU, motherfucker! Where are you now? Where are you now, bitch?! In the shit! In the fucking shit! I'm in the motherfucking *world*! YEEOWWEEE!!!"

"BILLY!" Dick was surprised to hear his own voice shouting at his nephew, who stopped in his tracks, laughing, and then panting and looking at him quizzically.

"What's wrong, Uncle Duck?"

Dick whispered hoarsely, "I have neighbors!"

Billy smiled and stage-whispered back, "Like a mile away!"

Dick shook his head. *There is a way this is done*, he thought. *There's a way you throw your ex-con nephew out of the house. But how?* He stepped forward and opened the screen door. Again, his voice was like a strangers' to him, slow and angry.

"This is my house!"

Billy wiped his sweaty face with his sleeves.

"Have you even gone upstairs? Have you looked at it? That's a work of fucking art up there!"

"I never asked you to do anything for me. I was happy the way things were."

"You were happy with this?!"

Billy pointed to the pile. Dick looked at the old toilet on its side like a discarded friend.

"Yes."

Billy turned away. "Oh, wow, man!" He bent backwards and shouted into the black sky, dense with stars, "FUUUUCK!" He turned and strode inside, past his uncle, through the kitchen, and up the stairs.

Dick could feel his heart, hear it almost. *This can't be right.* He could hear heavy-booted footfalls above him. The house seemed to shudder with the distinct sounds of packing upstairs. *This is real. It's happening.* He smiled. Footsteps on the stairs. He flushed with panic. His nephew pushed past him, duffle bag on his shoulder, and strode out through the kitchen door into the darkness. Dick followed and peered through the window above the sink, as Billy tossed his bag into his truck and climbed in. *Will it be this easy?* Outside, the engine started, headlights illuminated the trees, and two shiny eyes, low to the ground, blinked and vanished. Dick permitted himself to smile once more. That's when he looked up and saw Billy standing in front of him, shaking his head.

"You're a cold bastard, Uncle Duck," he said. "I never would have guessed it."

Uh, oh. How is this done? Dick looked down and away. "I miss my cat."

"Yeah, well, I miss my uncle."

Billy flung open the refrigerator and grabbed what was left of a six-pack of Coronas. Dick turned and retreated to the living room and sat in his chair, with his eyes on the floor. He could feel Billy standing in the kitchen, breathing. Then the screen door rattled, the truck door slammed, the engine roared, the gravel crunched and spit, and, suddenly, the night was alive with crickets. He waited a while, until he was certain that Billy was gone. Finally, he got up, shut the lights, and went upstairs.

He needed to pee before bed, so he crossed the hallway and peered inside the remodeled bathroom. He flipped on the light—*so bright!* – and stood there, astonished. The room shone. The tiles were white and the grouting free of mildew. The new fiberglass bathtub nestled in the alcove of clean lines and silver faucets. The floor was new. The toilet was squat and low, and

Dick decided to give it a try. So he dropped his shorts and sat, and it wasn't so bad after all. It felt like somebody else's house. But he could get used to it.

Every day, Dick found something new to admire. The brightness of the tiles, and how the sink reflected the morning light as he brushed his teeth. The wide wall-mirror that seemed to double the room. Little brass hooks with white rubber tips held his towels on the back of the door. Just enough. The sink was built into a cabinet, with drawers that slid easily. There was a little chrome towel rack to the right of the sink for his facecloth. He had never used a face cloth before, but now they became part of his routine. The silver toothbrush holder with six holes held his single, frayed toothbrush. There was thoughtfulness to the details, a rhythm. Where had Billy learned to do this, Dick had no idea, but he grew prouder of him every day. He was a natural. But the more he admired him, the guiltier he felt. Billy gave him this gift out of nothing but love. And he threw him out. How long would it take until Pete discovered what a selfish bastard he was? How long until he drove her away too?

Dick was on the toilet, thinking just those thoughts, when Solstice entered and demanded a petting at his feet. He was scratching his head when they heard the crackle of tires on the driveway. Solstice turned his ears and then jumped up. At first, Dick thought that it was a student arriving early, but his first appointment wasn't for two hours. *Billy?* He finished up and made his way downstairs and found Pete sitting at his kitchen table.

"Good morning, Richard."

He stopped and wrapped his flannel robe around him. She was dressed up in a pretty silk blouse and her hair was brushed and girlish. She wore lipstick. He was speechless.

"I was heading into Rochester, and I saw your house, and then I thought that I've been waiting like a schoolgirl for this bastard's phone call for over a week, and I am way beyond that in my life. Way beyond." She got up and filled the kettle and put it on the stove to boil. "Tea?"

Dick sat. He thought of words: *Trouble with Billy. Solstice. I'm sorry.* He tried to place them in his mouth but didn't have the breath to speak.

"So, I decided to let you off the hook and tell you that the offer has expired." She turned and sat across from him on the small, stained wooden table. She folded her hands before her. They were rough and creased: working hands. They were beautiful to him. His were bigger and fatter but, aside from the callused fingertips, smooth and feminine in comparison. Two- feet of table separated their hands, and he wondered, *Could I do it?*

"And then I thought, you idiot! You scared him away. A good, kind man, and you scared him away."

Billy would do it. Billy would be kissing her right now.

"You should have seen your face," she said, smiling at him. "Deer in the headlights." He looked up and tried to mirror her grin. He studied her pale blue eyes and thin lips and contrasted them in his mind with his big nose and ears and crooked teeth. *Why me?* It made no sense. The kettle began to whistle softly. He held her gaze. It was too much. She had pushed her chair back and turned to rise, when his hand leapt forward and, overreaching, grabbed her wrist. She looked down, placed her hand on top of his, turned it over, and cradled his big, warm palm in hers. The whistle grew louder. She grinned, raised his hand to her lips, kissed the palm, and then got up and turned off the stove. She took two mugs down from the cabinet. Richard saw poetry in her every movement as she poured their tea. When she spoke, it was easy, matter of fact.

"Billy's gone?"

"Hmnf."

"Solstice back?"

"Yeah."

22

"How's the bathroom?"

Richard thought, *A work of art.*

LUDMILLA THIS, LUDMILLA THAT

It was as if the light had found her face and he was seeing her for the first time.

"Monday?" Otto asked.

Pernille nodded and looked down into her empty cappuccino cup. She had broad cheeks, and her frizzy blonde hair was pulled back into a tight bun.

"For the summer?"

"The whole summer." Her blue eyes widened. She was from Denmark, but her accent could have been from anywhere east of the Rhine. "Till school. If I can afford it."

"That's . . ." He searched for the right word. He failed. "News."

"Good news?"

"Not so good."

"Good." She smiled. They faced each other across a small table in a trattoria on West Fourth Street, which was noticeably quieter now that the spring semester was over. "We should maybe do something together this weekend?" she ventured.

He shook his head with a pained grin.

"Maybe not?" she asked.

"Why Monday?"

"You're busy."

"I have a friend visiting."

"From London?" He felt a rush of shame. He had told her too much—way too much—about Ludmilla and London.

"She's married," he assured her. She raised her eyebrows. He sat up and put his hands on the table. "Yes, yes, of course. I'll text you when I know my schedule."

"If it's not inconvenient," she teased. Then she touched his hand with her fingertips. "Please."

Pernille's "Please" echoed in Otto's mind as he cleaned his studio apartment, just as Ludmilla's voice had played and replayed in his imagination for the past year and a half. Like, when she said, "You're going to screw up my life!" just before he kissed her in the cab. Those inconvenient intimacies threatened, for a few months, to disrupt her plans of escape and a new life.

He dragged the vacuum cleaner across the floor. Closed the futon back into a couch. Mopped and scrubbed the tiles of the bathroom. It was endless. But better to rush and worry than to sit and wait. It was hard to believe that, in a couple of hours, he would see her again. Hear her voice. Kiss her? That was unclear. But, at least, there would be no ocean between them. No Danny.

His phone shook. A text: *Landed*.

Ludmilla shut her phone, lousy with alerts, and gripped it in her lap. She looked out the airplane window during the long taxi to the terminal. *This is an ugly place*, she thought. She had imagined that the sight of New York would fill her with nostalgia and homecoming. But the anxiety she felt when boarding back at Heathrow seemed only to grow as the soot-gray grid had emerged below her. Her father, whose failing health and legal difficulties were the reason she was on this plane, was down there somewhere. As was her brother, Ron. Her ex-boyfriend Brian. Weak men, who wanted a piece of her. And Otto? She hoped that he was ready for friendship. Ludmilla fingered her wedding band. She had two passports but no home.

With the apartment cleaned, Otto climbed onto the fire escape, three stories above 17th Street, where the sunlight was warming into a perfect spring evening. He watched the street and waited. He had so many regrets about Ludmilla. Things he should have said. And not said. And done. And not done. He had been convinced that he loved her. He wasn't entirely sure now. He wanted her. Pernille was adorable, and his fingers still felt the charge of her touch this afternoon. But though his feelings were a jumble, it was as if his heart was arriving in a yellow cab when, curbed below him, the door opened, and Ludmilla stepped out in a bright green summer dress and straw hat, her long brown hair blowing about her face as she looked up and found him.

Ludmilla felt a small charge at the sight of Otto. She remembered that feeling, last year, or longer, when she had wanted to tell him all her secrets. That was the Otto she had missed the most. Not so much the clumsy would-be lover who bounded out the door and rushed to her with an awkward kiss that sent her hat askew.

"Oops, sorry. Hi," he said.

"Hi."

"I'll take that." He took her bag and led her inside.

Following him into his apartment, Ludmilla recognized the furniture, the movie posters, the jazz LPs, and the yellow stools by the small butcher's block table.

"Same shit, different place," said Otto.

"Nice," she said, noticing the single futon. "Is dad still paying for everything?"

"Dear old Dad."

Ludmilla crossed the room to the large window and looked out onto the leafy street. She felt his eyes on her and a pang of dread that staying here might be a mistake.

Having imagined her here for so long, it felt strange just to look at her. Thrilling. Otto had forgotten how tall she was—about his height. He wondered if he's ever seen her dressed in anything but black.

"How is dear old Dad?" she asked.

"I don't know. I haven't talked to him in a while. Which isn't great news." It was true—when Dad went quiet, it could only mean one thing: he was drunk or planning to be. "How's your old man?"

She grimaced.

"Are you going to see him when you are in town?"

"I'm afraid I have to."

"Why?"

"Apparently, he needs me. Go figure."

"I'm sorry to hear that. Do you want a beer?"

She turned to him. "I think our dads would like that."

Otto pulled two beers from his small refrigerator and opened them. He handed her a bottle and sat on the futon. "Here's to our two dads."

They clinked necks and drank. Ludmilla scanned the room and then turned to him.

"Otto . . ."

"You're here! I can't believe you're here!" His giddiness made her pull inward.

"It's surreal." She sat on the edge of the futon.

"What time is it?" he asked. She squinted at him. "In your head?"

"Oh, I have no idea. Ten o'clock? Eleven? I'm fucking exhausted."

"How's London?"

"I don't want to say."

"Why?"

"Because you are going to say . . ."

"What?"

"That I made a mistake. But I didn't. It's just hard."

He smiled. She shook her head.

"How's Danny?" Otto asked.

"Danny's fine."

"He called me a wanker."

"It's a term of affection."

"I know what it means. The feeling's mutual. Are you acting?"

Here it comes. He's happiest when I'm miserable. "Some. Not much. I'm sick of it anyway. Squatting sucks. Everyone drinks. . . . But at least there's the fine weather." She smiled and took a drink.

He sat up. "You're a wonderful actress. You should be modeling."

"My face is too fat."

"Bullshit."

"That's what I'm told." She'd heard that more than once. It came as a relief—*you can't be an actress if the camera hates your face.*

"You're beautiful. You should be in New York."

"There's nothing for me in New York."

"*I'm* in New York."

She turned away. *That was fast.* She stood. "Where's your bathroom?"

He pointed down the hall. "Over there," he said. "Are you hungry?"

"Starving. Suddenly."

Otto and Ludmilla crossed Union Square, verdant and crowded in the evening sun. His hand brushed hers and she withdrew. A year ago, the rules of touching were clear. What were they now? Even Ludmilla didn't know. She had gotten married for the UK residency, but lately, it had started to feel almost real. Danny surprised her with his kindness and seriousness about the marriage. Fully engaged with his band, he didn't crowd her. He *was* furious when she told him that she would stay at Otto's. He demanded her promise to be faithful. She gave it. She meant it. But when Otto put his arm around her shoulder, she let him. She even put her hand on his skinny waist. He pulled her close. They looked like lovers walking into the Union Square Café.

They fell into easy conversation over dinner, finding comfort in each other's company. And Ludmilla, against her better judgement, found herself revealing too much of her doubts and difficulties. It put Otto in a superior position, which she resented but also kind of enjoyed, because it was so familiar.

"It was the only way I could stay in the country," she explained. "We went to the pub, had a few pints with our friends, and just went and did it."

"How did you feel about it?"

"I was nervous! When the time came to take the vows, I started coughing and couldn't stop. I could hardly get through it." She laughed. He shook his head and joined her, although the image stung.

"And that was it. Married." She waved her ringed hand and then lifted her glass and sipped her wine. It was a simple gold band, but to Otto, it was the ugliest ring he'd ever seen.

"But why? I still don't understand why you had to do it."

"To stay in England. To work."

"No. Why you had to leave New York."

"I had to."

"Why?"

"I was miserable in New York."

"Who isn't?" His voice had a tone of accusation. He heard it too and backtracked with a smile. "That's what makes it work."

Ludmilla traced the rim of her wine glass with her index finger. She was tired of explaining herself. In her body, she felt the sense-memory of sadness. "A few months before we met," she said, keeping her eyes down, "I never told you this. I checked myself into Bellevue for a few hours . . . I couldn't stop crying. I was thinking . . . *bad thoughts.*"

Otto leaned forward. Her face, now lit by candlelight and room light, glowed warmly.

"Then Brian was pressuring me to get back together. My dad was calling for money. My brother was using again. No work. Spending down my inheritance. For what? I had friends in London. It was a total break." She took a sip of wine and sat back.

"What about me?" he asked. She smiled softly.

"Well, you came along and made things . . ." For a second, Ludmilla thought, maybe she could unwind this and not go there. She was not ready to name what she felt—*felt, past tense*—over a year ago. And if she could not name what it was, how could she explain how it changed?

"What?"

"Complicated."

Otto beamed. "I did?" Ludmilla nodded, as he sat up. "Tell me I did!"

"You did," she reassured him. "I didn't want it to go any further. I couldn't handle it."

He sat back, savoring. "I *did*." Their eyes met. "But not complicated enough."

"Otto, this may be difficult for you to believe. But my leaving New York had *nothing* to do with you."

"You said, 'Maybe you are the love of my life.' And then you *left*."

Ludmilla threw up her hands and shrugged.

"What if I was? What if I *am*?"

"More wine?" Ludmilla reached for the wine bottle and refilled their glasses. She took a big, long gulp and felt the deep red warmth flow through her.

Otto shook his head, his anger rising. "I thought you were a coward."

"It's good wine."

"Ludmilla."

"Go fuck yourself." She took another big sip, set her glass down, and looked at him. "It took a hell of a lot more courage for me to leave than it would have taken for me to stay."

He looked into her eyes: bright green, deadly serious, impenetrable. There were times when he had looked at these same eyes and thought, *I know this woman.* At other times, like this, he knew he never would. And he certainly wasn't going to talk her into anything she didn't want to do.

"I'm a drag, right?" he said, finally. "You left because I'm such a bummer."

Ludmilla laughed. "That's right. I moved to London and married Danny because you *harshed* my mellow."

Otto shook his head and joined her laughter. "You were such a shit to me," he said, suddenly feeling free to speak his mind.

"Really?!" She kind of liked this Otto.

"You stood me up."

"*Once!*"

"I was so fucking pissed at you. You led me on. And then you refused to sleep with me."

"You had your chance."

"When?"

"You know when."

Ouch. It was true. *That kiss in the cab.* Why didn't he invite her in? He sent her home, feeling chivalrous and confident. It was the last time they wanted the same thing at the same time. Otto drained his glass. "This is good wine. Let's have another bottle of this." He spied the passing waitress and signaled to her, lifting the bottle, and shaking it.

"You're just trying to get me drunk and take advantage of me," Ludmilla teased.

"Let me know how I'm doing! I'd hate to miss another chance!"

Otto's phone buzzed in his pocket. He took it out and saw a text from Pernille: *LUNCH SAT?* Ludmilla could see his face change.

"Who's that?" she asked.

Otto took a breath and pocketed his phone.

"A girl."

"A girl with a name?"

"Pernille Bjorn Something. She's Danish. She's crazy about me. She sexts me day and night."

"Ooh, la, la!"

"Yes, I may score with the frequency of Halley's Comet, but I choose well."

They laughed as the waitress presented a new bottle of wine. They watched each other as the bottle was opened and poured.

The dim apartment seemed smaller to Ludmilla as they entered.

"You don't know the whole story, Otto," she said. "As usual, you have your own version."

Otto dropped his keys on the butcher's block and turned on a standing lamp. "Yeah, alone in a restaurant. Feeling like a chump. What am I missing?" he demanded.

"What I was going through!" She collapsed onto the futon.

"Do you want a beer?"

"No, please. The wine." The room wasn't spinning, but she could feel the alcohol and her jet lag throughout her body like a weight. She put her head back. "I called you back," she said. "You came over. *We kissed*. It was kind of a date. I only missed dinner."

Otto sat next to her. "That was so humiliating: sitting in your room, watching you pack. You were throwing out all this personal stuff. Things from your mother. I couldn't believe how cold you were about it."

"It was junk."

"You invited your fucking roommate into your room so that you wouldn't have to be alone with me."

"He was a great guy. I wanted you to meet him." She felt a wave of exhaustion. "I'm tired."

"I vibed him. He left, finally."

Ludmilla let out a sigh and leaned forward. "So, is this where we're sleeping? How do you . . .?"

Otto waved for her to stand up and began to pull on the futon frame. "But then we kissed," he continued. "And you said that thing you said."

"I don't remember saying that."

Otto struggled with the futon, slipped, and then fell back into its fold.

Ludmilla laughed. "Do you need a hand?"

"I got it." He rolled on the floor and yanked the frame forward, until it fell flat with a loud thump. He crawled onto it and lay on his back. He looked up to see her smiling down at him.

"I keep a journal, Ludmilla. I wrote it all down."

"You did?"

Otto reached over to his bookshelf and pulled out a thick, black sketchbook and opened it. Across the pages, the thin, barely decipherable lines of his handwriting stretched to the margins. Ludmilla felt cornered.

"That's weird."

"What's weird about keeping a journal?"

She sat at the corner of the futon-bed. "It's just. I dunno. I never saw the point." She could think of nothing more horrid than a *written record* of her life. Otto flipped through the pages.

"OK, where are you, Ludmilla Svoboda?" he said. "Here you are."

"I'm afraid."

"We meet. You act in my movie. Blah, blah, blah. You call me. We get drinks. We *kiss* . . ." He flipped several pages. "Let's see . . . Ludmilla this, Ludmilla that . . ."

She smiled warily as she looked over his shoulder. She couldn't read his writing—except to see her name capitalized and repeated on page after page.

"Here it is. *January 20, 2008.*" He cleared his throat theatrically and read, "*I watched her pack. Partly loving her. Partly dying. Partly feeling strong. Partly feeling like the chump of the year. She's beautiful. She's funny. And she's going to London on Friday. Forever. It was time to go.*"

Ludmilla sat back. Otto's voice lowered as he read on. "*She said, 'Where are you going?' 'Home,' I said. 'I can't stay here. This is not good for me.' We kissed. And she said, 'What if you are the love of my life?' And she looked at me. And then she looked off.*" Otto stopped reading and turned to her. Ludmilla looked down.

"That's not fair," she said.

He closed the journal and moved closer to her. "Why?"

"I'm not saying . . ." she hesitated. "I'm not saying I didn't *feel* that. I just don't remember saying it out loud."

She looked at him. For a moment, his hazel eyes brought her into the past with him, and she felt the same sadness and the same pull, of when Otto appeared as a new possibility, of when she could imagine herself folding into and being bounded by his life. He touched her cheek and laced her hair with his fingers. She looked down, and he kissed her temple, and the sweet scent of her filled him. And she felt comforted, as he kissed her eyebrow and her cheek. But even when she was infatuated with him, she knew that, for all his bravado, his affection, his scorn, and his scolding, he was a boy. And she was his fantasy. And besides, she made a promise to Danny. When he kissed her lips, she recoiled.

"What are you doing?" she asked.

"I'm kissing you about the face and neck," he said, leaning into her cheek. She pulled away.

"Otto!"

"What?"

"I'm married!"

He froze. "No, you're not."

"Yes, I am!"

He shook his head dismissively. "You're . . . green-card married. Or whatever color it is in England."

They stared at each other for a moment. He reached for her again, and she stood up. "I can't believe you!"

"What can't you believe?" He rolled back on his elbows, studying her. "Ludmilla, you know how I feel."

"We're *friends*."

He held her gaze. "I know you feel it too."

"No, you don't. You don't know how I feel. You have this idea of me. You write it down like it's real." She felt a surge of shame and panic.

"It's what *happened*."

"It's what happened *to you*! Fuck! I need to call Danny."

"You what?"

"I promised him I'd call." She fetched her phone from her purse.

"Now? You need to call him now? What time is it over there?"

"He said to call anytime."

"It's four in the morning or something."

"He's my husband," she said. The sharp British *ring-ring, ring-ring* filtered into her ear. Suddenly, there was Danny's sleepy "Yeh?" loud and clear. Not so distant at all.

"Hi, it's me. Did I wake you?" Otto watched in disbelief, as she cradled the phone to her ear and turned away, her voice lowered in intimacy. "I'm at Otto's. It's cool. I miss you."

Otto didn't remember falling asleep. In fact, the night seemed endless, his thoughts swirling as Ludmilla quietly snored beside him. It brought back a memory from college, of when he drove to Boston to win back his girlfriend, Jan. That also did not go as planned. They ended up sleeping side by side in her stifling room, his body wracked with heartache and rejection. He vowed he would never put himself in that position again—to share a bed with a woman who refused to sleep with him. And here he was.

Waking up, he saw the back of Ludmilla's head beside him, and the sting of last night's humiliation overcame him. How could she be *right there* and lost to him at the same time? He sat up. It was early. He had to get out of there.

Otto sipped his coffee and stared at an uneaten corn muffin on a plate in front of him. The diner was nearly empty and buzzed quietly with plate clinks and soft chatter. He opened his journal and tried to piece together the events of the night before . . . tried to put it into a narrative that made sense. It didn't. Ludmilla didn't make sense. Unless he was completely wrong about everything. And that thought sent a chill through him. Was he wrong about everybody? What about Pernille?

He took out his phone, and her text from last night floated in a green tile on the screen saver. LUNCH SAT?

He swiped it open and typed, *YES!*

Ludmilla woke up with a start. Panic gripped her briefly, until the room took shape around her. The intercom trilled from a box by the door. She looked beside her. No Otto. *Relief.* She rose and stumbled toward the door and hit the talk button.

"Who . . . ?"

"It's me. I locked myself out," came Otto's mechanical voice. She buzzed him in. She had to pee. She opened the door and heard Otto's footsteps on the stairs below. Arriving on the landing, he approached her, brought his face close to hers and growled.

She growled back.

When she came out of the bathroom, Otto was seated on a yellow stool with a muffin in his hand.

"Where were you?" she asked.

"I went to get some breakfast."

"By yourself?"

"You were asleep." He handed her the muffin. "Here." She took it, sniffed it, and placed it on the butcher's block. He watched her. "Can I ask you something?"

"Sure."

"Remember that night, in the cab, when we kissed for the first time?"

Ludmilla sighed and sat down. "Oh, Otto."

"Would you have come home with me if I asked you?"

She looked at him. "I don't know. I was pretty drunk. It was almost two years ago." She remembered the kiss, a sense of falling, of surrender. "I wondered why you didn't."

"Was *that* it? Was that the moment I had my chance?" Ludmilla shrugged softly. "Would it have changed anything?" he asked.

"I don't know. Maybe. Maybe not." She could picture him kissing her and then stepping back and closing the cab door, grinning and proud. She could see that he was lost in that moment now. "Why didn't you?"

"I thought I had time." He smiled softly. "And you scared me a little."

"I was pretty set in my plans. It would have . . ."

"What?"

She considered. "Made it harder."

"This is easy?" He smiled weakly.

She tilted her head at Otto, who sat glumly across from her. *It wasn't a mistake, after all.*

"Thanks for the muffin," she said, rising.

Pernille smiled brightly at Otto as she opened the gate under the stairs to her garden apartment. "Otto!"

"Hi."

"Come." She led him. "Do you want lunch?"

"Not right now," said Otto. "I'm a little hungover actually."

"Iced tea?"

"Water."

Pernille walked to the kitchen. Otto followed her slowly. The apartment was in a state of shedding its current inhabitants—open drawers and cabinets and two large suitcases agape on the floor of her bedroom. He wanted desperately to match her sunniness, to lose the gloom that had followed him to Brooklyn. But he was sleepy, and sharp waves of a headache stung him above his right eyebrow.

"How is packing going?"

"Terrible!" she called back from the kitchen. "I have so much stuff! How did I get so much stuff in less than a year with no money?"

She brought him a glass of water.

"Thanks."

"You're welcome!" Pernille turned to her bed, piled with laundry, and began folding blouses and sweaters and packing them into her suitcase. Otto sat on a wicker chair and sipped the cold water and watched her. She wore a loose-fitting light-yellow T-shirt and baggy cotton pants. Bare feet. Without looking up, she asked, "How's your friend?"

"Fine."

"Big night?"

"No."

"But you are hungover."

"Very."

"Did you have fun?"

"Are you trying to ask me something?"

She smiled as she stuffed a short stack of sweaters into the open case. "Maybe."

Pernille's "Maybe," like yesterday's "Please," warmed him. Her openness was uncomplicated. With Ludmilla, everything was complicated. As he watched Pernille, he thought, *Could I love this woman?* At least he could reassure her with the truth. "Nothing happened. In a big way."

"Good." Pernille picked up a large, clear plastic bag and began stuffing stacks of notebooks and school papers inside. It reminded him of Ludmilla throwing away her mother's things. She turned to a small bookshelf. "So many books! I can't take any of you with me. Why did I take 19th-Century British Literature?" She pulled an orange-spined paperback from the shelf and dropped it into the bag. "I hate you D. H. Lawrence! You have mommy issues!" She grabbed two more. "I hate you, George Eliot! Admit you're a girl!" Dropping them as well, she pulled a thick volume. "And I really hate you, William Thackeray. You bored me to *tears!*" Pernille plucked a row of books and tossed them in the bag.

Otto did not know why, but the sight of her discarding books filled him with disgust. "You are throwing them out?" he asked.

"Recycling."

Otto eyed a cardboard box on the floor. Putting down his water, he fetched it and crossed over to her. He picked the books out of the trash bag and placed them in the box.

"What are you doing?" Pernille asked.

"They don't throw books out in Brooklyn." He pointed to the remaining books on the shelf. "All these?"

"Those. But not these." She pulled several volumes and cradled them. Otto swept the rest into the box with a growing agitation. He then lifted the box and walked out the front door. She put down her rescued volumes on her bed and followed. Otto placed the paperbacks on the steps of the brownstone, covers facing out. Pernille stepped out and watched.

"There," he said, adjusting the books for visibility. "Now. These will be gone by tomorrow. Brooklyn will take them, and they won't be turned into paper towels."

He stood back. Pernille's smile was gone. "Thank you," she said.

"Even William Thackeray may find a friend. Stranger things have happened." He forced a smile, which she echoed faintly. His phone buzzed in his pocket. He took it out and saw a text from Ludmilla: *CAFE REGGIO 2:30?*

Pernille turned to go back inside.

"Listen," said Otto, apologetically.

She stopped, looking at her pink toes on the blue-slate step. "London?"

He flushed with shame. "I just . . ."

"Go."

"I can call you later?"

She stepped down and closed the gate behind her.

Back at his apartment, Otto paged through his journal. Like every girl before her, Ludmilla appeared first as an offhand reference, a curiosity. Then, within a few pages, her name appeared again, and then reappeared in greater frequency, until the pages were filled with Ludmillas. He looked for the narrative of their intimacy, for proof. Mostly, it appeared, they argued about why she shouldn't go to London and why she should sleep with him. But there was that time when they made out in her bedroom. When London went away. He held her and stroked her hair, and her green eyes opened to him. Once or twice, he thought, she showed him her heart.

But there was no narrative of Otto and Ludmilla, no real story that he could see. Just a jumble of scenes, maybe a half-dozen different Ludmillas and the written record of Otto's growing confusion, missteps, and ambivalence. It was only after she left that he was able to shape the memories into a love story that was destined to resume. All those letters. And when she announced her trip to New York, he believed that she was coming back *for him*, because, after all, she said *that thing* on which he built all his fantasies. *That thing* that she didn't remember saying.

It was nearly two in the afternoon; time to leave to meet her in the West Village. He thought ahead to another night of hurt and thwarted desire. He looked down at her duffle bag on the floor, her toothbrush sticking out. He stuffed it in and zipped it closed.

After a painful morning with Brian—another man who insisted that he loved her and she loved him—Ludmilla was exhausted and stressed and thirty minutes late when she made it to the café where Otto was sitting at an outside table, pouting into an empty cup.

"Hey, sorry," she said, as she sat across from him.

"How's Brian?"

Ludmilla gave an exaggerated shiver. "Oh, not good. I thought it would be easy to fuck him over, but it wasn't. He took it bad. We were together for five years."

"Didn't you break a bottle over his head?"

"*Once.*" Ludmilla looked down to find her bag at Otto's feet. "Why is my bag here?"

Otto took a breath. "You can't stay with me."

"Why?"

"I can't do that again."

"You're kicking me out because I won't have sex with you?"

"I can't share my bed with you if I can't touch you. It's not fair of you to ask me to."

Ludmilla felt a surge of anger. "What an asshole you are! Where am I going to stay tonight?"

"You'll figure something out."

"Didn't I say I wouldn't sleep with you? Why can't you respect that? If someone said that to me, I'd respect it."

"You said . . ."

"*Fuck* what I said. That was a year and a half ago. I've moved on. You should too. I think you just need someone, and so you happened to choose me."

Otto winced.

Once, his pout would have aroused her pity. But no more. She was done with men—*boys*—and their plans for her life.

"Otto, I'm married. I live in London. Did you think I was going to leave Danny and move back to New York to be with you?"

"I didn't expect to see you again. You called *me*."

"Because we're *friends*."

Ouch. "We're something, Ludmilla, but we're not friends. Certainly not lovers. But we're something. And the worst part is . . ."

"What?"

He looked at her, staring impatiently at him. He loved her face, even now. "The worst part is, I like you more now than I remembered. I mean," he forced a smile. "Not at this particular moment, but . . ." Ludmilla's eyes softened. He leaned forward. "Forget about me for a second. You complain about your career. But London is not the solution. Being somebody's wife? You're making a mistake."

"Well, that's your default position, isn't it?" she snapped. "I'm fucking up my life if I'm not fucking you."

Otto stopped himself. "So, there's nothing between us?"

"Not like that."

He stared at her.

"What are you thinking?" she asked.

"I'm thinking I don't recognize you."

"This is me." She held up her hands, like she was an open book. "You should call the Dutch girl."

"The Dane."

"The *Dane*. Sorry."

"She's leaving tomorrow for Copenhagen for the summer. Or forever."

Ludmilla laughed. "Boy, can you pick 'em!"

Otto rose suddenly, almost stumbling out of his chair. He opened his wallet and dropped some dollars on the table. Crossing over to her, he cupped his hand on her cheek and looked into her eyes, trying to freeze her face into his memory. She leaned into his warm hand. And although they felt differently, they were both certain that this was the last time they would ever see each other.

He growled at her.

She growled back.

He stroked her hair and walked away.

The D train emerged from the tunnel onto the Manhattan Bridge. Otto stood by the door in the partly empty car with his phone to his ear. When he heard her voice, he nearly shouted, "Pernille! I'm sorry!"

Pernille sat on her bed. "For what?"

"I'm sorry for the way I behaved. I'm sorry for blowing you off this weekend."

"You were where you wanted to be," she said.

The girders of the bridge flew by in the angled light over the East River. "Listen, I'm on the bridge. I'm going to get cut off. Can I see you?"

"You just saw me."

Otto pressed his head against the glass. "I need to see you before you go away. I need to know something before you go away." He waited for her voice. "Pernille?"

She cleared her throat.

"What is there to know?"

"How you feel. How I feel."

"How can we know that?"

The train was approaching Brooklyn. "Pernille?"

She sat in the afternoon light in her clean room with her packed bags. "I'm very busy."

"Can I see . . . ?"

"I don't think . . ."

"Just for a minute . . . ?" The car darkened around him. "Pernille. I'm going into a tunnel . . . Pernille?" He looked at his phone as the last bar vanished and the call ended. Glancing up, he saw his fellow passengers staring at him. He dropped into a seat and turned his face to the window. In the scratched glass, Otto saw his darkened reflection: shaken, a shadow, a shade.

BUNNY

Just like that, Bunny was gone. And with her, every hope Gladys had of peace and home. Just a week before, they were all celebrating and singing at Hal Lanigan's surprise birthday party. Now, she rang him at his office at the *Great Neck News*.

"Hal? Glad Verga."

"Oh, darling," said Hal. "Everyone is in shock. How's Jack?"

"He's a wreck," she said. "What can we do?"

"About what?"

"Does this have to make the press?"

"Oh, Glad. Jack Olney is the mayor. It's already out. Promise me you won't read the New York papers."

Gladys's mind was swimming. "What can we do?"

"I'll put something in the News tomorrow."

"Not an obit. She deserves something more . . ."

"A tribute," he offered.

Gladys caught her breath.

"A tribute, yes."

"I'll get quotes," Hal said. "Annie adored her."

"Gene Buck. Call Gene. He loved her."

"You sure?"

"Yes. Call the big shots. She was the mayor's wife for Christ's sake."

The News was a local paper, but it had influence. Hal was a darling of the theater people who mattered, and his paper catered to their society ambitions. Gladys had worked so hard to be accepted into their world, especially since leaving vaudeville—and her husband—and coming East to help Jack with Bunny nine months ago. Gene Buck was a Ziegfeld Follies producer. He was charmed by Gladys's younger sister and also flirted with Gladys last summer. He played the piano while Gladys sang "Crying For You," which she had made popular in '23. *Why not a solo act?* And Hal's birthday was so gay, and Bunny's laughter was a birdsong above the happy chatter. Her shyness melted away. Both Jack and Gladys hoped that Bunny had finally turned a corner. But today, Gladys wondered if her joy that night was because she had already decided to release herself from her terrors, from the concerns of others.

Gladys called Western Union and sent telegrams to her brothers—Bobby in Birmingham and Arty in Davenport (she hoped). Her voice shook as she dictated the message.

"FLORENCE DEAD STOP." What else was there to say? She was not about to say how. What did she want from them? Telephone? Come East? The line clicked with static while the operator waited.

"Is that all, ma'am?"

"Yes. Thank you. Charge it to Manhasset Five-Four."

"One dollar and twenty cents to Manhasset Five-Four. Very good."

Gladys sat for a moment in the kitchen. Jack had slept on the couch and left early without a word. Her ears rang in the silence of the house, which still seemed to echo the vibrations of yesterday's tragedy. She stood, wrapped a shawl around her shoulders, and stepped out into the rose garden—always her sanctuary. It was a cold November morning. The trees were almost bare, and the petals were wilted into tiny fists, drained of color. Although she wanted to keep her mind on Bunny, she could not help but think that her life was suddenly unmoored. Yesterday, this was her home. Today, she was a houseguest. Last winter, she was married and a star of vaudeville. Today, she was separated, unemployed, and dependent. Yesterday, she had a little sister who needed her. Today . . . She shivered in the stiff wind.

Jack Olney had rescued them both in 1920. They were all living in the same apartment building on West 145th Street in Morningside Heights. Gladys had brought Flo (she was not yet Bunny) and their mother, Emmah, from Iowa to New York the year before. Her plan was to sing. She had begun with amateur nights in Waterloo and had appeared on bills in the Pantages circuit. New York made sense. Except it didn't. Emmah hated it and fell into a deep despondency. Flo, always anxious, followed her mother, and Gladys found herself being the caretaker of them both in a strange city where they knew no one. Then Jack met Flo on the front steps of their building one morning. Soon, the shy, nervous little Florence became sunny, flighty Bunny, desperately in love with the young banker. When she became Mrs. Jack Olney the following year, Gladys was freed to travel to stages grand and crummy. And sing. The following year, she shared a bill with Niccolò Verga, the Newsboy Caruso, who was famous for his beautiful tenor voice and his comic character of an off-the-boat Italian. They married and built an act of comedy and songs that carried them all over the country.

Even though she'd met plenty of veterans and had heard their stories, life in vaudeville was harder than Gladys had expected. She and Nick traveled nonstop, jumping from one small town to another. They never had top billing, but they never opened a show and they never closed one. Usually, they preceded the headliner, and, over nine years, they built a reputation among critics and the dwindling audiences. They performed the same act, sometimes four times a day. They were always broke. And Nick was always disappearing with some young thing. Eventually, those few moments on stage when Gladys could sing were not enough. When Jack, Bunny, and their mother moved to Long Island and built this house—a tidy white colonial in the new development of Plandome Heights—Gladys envied the anchor it seemed to give them. When Emmah died in '26, Gladys and Nick were at the height of their popularity. She could barely make the funeral. It was clear to her that Bunny was devastated and terrified that her own spells were like their mother's. She spent weeks in bed. Jack, whose career at Salomon was taking off with the market, was concerned enough to put her under Dr. Evers's care, for all the good that did. When Jack cabled Gladys last February, asking her to come East to help with Bunny, she was ready to make a home.

The *Great Neck News* office bustled with activity in anticipation of the week's printing deadline. Hal Lanigan seemed surprised to see Gladys in his office but rose and hugged her anyway.

"Did you reach Gene?" she asked.

"Yes. He sends his condolences. Said, he never met a finer lady in his life."

"Is that all?"

He waved her to sit and handed her the typewritten copy paper.

"Here, I just . . ."

"Thank you, Hal."

He sat at his desk. Gladys read:

BUNNY OLNEY

As dear and as lovely a little woman as ever lived was
Mrs. Jack Olney of Plandome Road, Plandome, whose
suicide last Thursday stunned her many friends.

"Death," she said.

He looked at her.

"'Whose *death* last Thursday stunned her many friends.'"

"Fine. Right."

She read on:

> Bunny was a sweet little soul. She was scarcely thirty
> and had a husband who was devoted to her, and she
> had everything to live for. But she was of a very nervous
> disposition, could never forget how her dear Mother had
> suffered, and always said that she would never bring the
> like worries to those who cared for her.

She looked up at him.

"How did you know?"

"I pay attention. It's what I do."

She scanned the page one more time. It was strange to see her sister's life summed up in so few words. Hal described the parties they attended last week and the prominent guests in true News fashion. And Gene Buck's disappointing quote. But where was Bunny? Where was Florence Gwenllian Williams de Olney, born, like her, in Valparaíso, Chile, daughter of missionaries, and abandoned, along with her mother and brothers and sister, by their father? Where was her sweet sister, who was shivering with her in that first Iowa winter, speaking Spanish together to the astonishment and mockery of their classmates in that tiny, dirty town? Where was Little Flo, who lacked her sister's moxie, who wanted only to cheer her mother up and then later to make a home and be Jack's Bunny? Where were the children they wanted but could never have?

She stared at the page until the letters began to blur and shift. She looked up, and Hal was watching her. "It needs a stronger ending," she said.

"I'll take another pass."

Gladys sat for a moment.

"God never took to a sweeter soul than Bunny. Something like that. And no mention of suicide. Please."

"Of course. You should get some rest."

Driving back, Gladys felt her anger surging. *Get some rest!* That's all any of those men ever had to offer. Wasn't that what that idiot Dr. Evers told Bunny over and over for a year? He gave her powders and told her to rest her nerves. As if she could sleep off her pain. And month after month, Bunny only got more anxious, more agitated. Even Jack, who could see with his own eyes how little the good doctor's care helped, kept calling him back, kept trusting his counsel. *Men!* It was Gladys who said, no, let's go out, let's see people. And Bunny would delay and cry and complain and resist but would inevitably be the sweetest, most charming young lady, with her laughter like music, and be showered with compliments that made Gladys a little jealous. Because it wasn't Gladys's voice or her stage career that gave her entry to those rooms, it was her pretty little sister, the young mayor's wife.

Back home. No Jack. But a half-dozen telegrams of condolences were on the floor of the foyer, mostly addressed to Mayor John S. Olney. The one for her was from Birmingham:

DEVASTATED AT NEWS BOBBY TRAVELING WILL
CONTACT FATHER SEND FUNERAL DETAILS
LOVE AND DEEPEST SYMPATHY = RUTH.

Thank God for Ruth, Bobby's young wife. Gladys wasn't sure she liked her at first—she had met her share of phony Southern belles in her travels. But maybe Ruth was OK. Gladys was relieved for not having to telegram her father in Ecuador. She placed the envelopes on the table in the foyer and climbed the stairs. When she reached the landing, she saw that the door to Bunny and Jack's bedroom was ajar. Her knees shook gently as she reached the top of the stairs and pushed the door open. The bed had been made. The carpet had been removed and the wood floor in front of the dresser was cleaned. Jack must have done this. She stepped into the room and saw herself in the mirror over the dresser. Her eyes were red and puffy, and her hair, a tangle. Had she really gone out like that? She sat on the bed.

Two days earlier, Gladys woke up to the sounds of Bunny crying. She rose in the early morning darkness, put on her robe, and crossed the hallway. Jack, half-dressed for work, sat on the bed, stroking his wife's short hair as she lay clutching her pillow.

"Talk to me, darling. Tell me," he pleaded.

When Jack looked up at Gladys, she could see his exhaustion and desperation. He stood up as she took his place and put her arms around her sister.

"She just woke up like this," he said.

Gladys whispered in Bunny's ear. "*¿Que pasó, Cariña? Digame. ¿Por qué estás llorando?*"

"I have to go in," Jack said.

"Go. I'll stay with her."

Jack went downstairs. Bunny turned her face to Gladys. Her eyes were red and wet. It was the same look her mother had when a storm of fear would overtake her. Florence had the same wide-set green eyes, thick eyebrows, and high forehead as Emmah, as Gladys, as Bobby, but she also had her father's broad nose and pale Welsh skin. The whole family was in her face. She was terrified. Gladys stroked her forehead.

"Florita."

The night before, they had been out to a women-only gathering at Annie and Hal Lanigan's. Bunny was less lively than she had been at Hal's birthday party last Saturday. While Annie tried to keep things upbeat, there was a lot of talk about the market crash the month before and rumors of fortunes lost and fears for the future. Gladys could see Bunny withdrawing little by little as the evening wore on. When Hal stopped by to pay his respects, Gladys took the opportunity to say good night and she and Bunny motored him back to the News office. As usual, Hal had lots of gossip about their famous neighbors—Eddie Cantor and Ring Lardner—which they all enjoyed, especially the details he couldn't print. But he, too, was worried. Something was coming to an end, but he couldn't say what.

Gladys managed to get Bunny up and dressed and out for a walk in the crisp fall air. The neighborhood was new, with houses and empty lots spaced apart. Tall oak trees, speckled with orange and yellow leaves, towered over the bare saplings on newly planted lawns. Her plan was to keep Bunny moving. There was cleaning to do. They could practice some songs. They would go to town and shop and make a dinner for Jack tonight. Anything but rest.

"I'm worried about Jack," Bunny said.

"Don't be," Gladys said. "Salomon is mostly bonds. They're probably making money on all this." It sounded good, but no one really knew what was happening. They could both see the worry in Jack's face. He'd been working day and night.

"I'm a disappointment to him."

"No! He loves you."

"I am. I am. And you should be singing and not be stuck here with me."

"I'll be singing again soon."

"I've let you all down."

"Bunny!"

"I know it. It's OK." Bunny turned to her and smiled. "I know it."

When they returned to the house, Bunny went to her room and closed the door. This was not unusual. Gladys checked on her throughout the day. She did a quick shop in town, and when she pulled into the driveway, she thought she saw Bunny through the windows, crossing the living room from Jack's study. When she walked in, she heard the bedroom door shut upstairs. She went up and pushed the door open. Bunny was curled on the bed with her eyes open.

"Are you hungry?" Gladys asked.

Bunny shook her head.

"I'm going to prepare a nice roast for Jack. Will you come down and help me?" Bunny didn't respond. Gladys sat beside her. "What are you thinking about?"

"I said the wrong thing."

"When?"

"At Annie's."

"What did you say?"

Bunny turned her face into the pillow. *"Dije algo incorrecto. Siempre digo lo incorrecto."*

"¿Cuándo? ¿A quien?"

"Nada. Olvidalo."

The phone rang sharply downstairs, startling Gladys. She stroked her sister's cheek. *"No te preocupes."*

It was Jack on the phone.

"How is she?"

"In bed."

"Sleeping?"

"No."

"What do you think?"

"I've seen this play before." It sounded cold to her own ears as Gladys said it, but it was true. Her mother had stayed in bed for nearly a year. And Bunny had been having days like these even before Gladys came to stay with them. Dr. Evers called it a "nervous breakdown," whatever that meant. Bunny just seemed sad. It was as if she was the guardian of everyone's sadness. As if she could free them all to be happy. But it didn't work that way. And Bunny knew it. And that made it worse.

"It's a bit mad around here," said Jack. "I'll try to get home as early as I can."

Gladys roasted a chicken with potatoes and carrots—Jack's favorite—for dinner. At seven, when he did not show up, she knew that he would be working late. And Bunny would not come down. Gladys ate alone in the kitchen, without much appetite.

After washing up, Gladys walked into the living room and sat at the spinet piano. She had recently purchased some sheet music with an idea to find new songs to perform. Music was changing, getting faster. Songs like "Crying For You" were old hat. Her voice was old hat. She liked the new singers, like Bessie Smith and Fats Waller, but she couldn't imagine herself singing "Ain't Misbehavin'." She bought the music anyway and opened it. She smiled at the dense clusters of notes and tricky notation. Her fingers fumbling, she made her way slowly through the opening measures and, sight-reading, softly sang the prologue that she had not heard on the record.

Though it's a fickle age

With flirting all the rage

Here's one bird with self-control

Happy inside my cage.

That wasn't very good. She turned the page to the main verse, her left hand finding the "stride" base note and chord pattern that created the rhythm.

No one to talk with, all by myself

No one to walk with, but I'm happy on the shelf.

Ain't misbehavin', saving all my love for you!

She heard a creak on the stairs and turned, and there was Bunny, seated, peering through the railings. Her hands lifted from the keys.

"Play!" said Bunny.

"I can't sing this."

"How would Nick sing it?"

Gladys smiled, puffed her chest, and imitated her husband's stage-Italian accent and deep tenor.

"Still Meesbehavin',

Breaking all-a my a-vows to you!"

Bunny laughed, and Gladys felt a surge of relief. She patted the piano bench, and Bunny rose slowly and joined her. Playing and singing together was something they had done since childhood. Emmah was a piano teacher, and she instilled a love of music in them both and supported Gladys's ambitions to perform. Flo was too shy to sing for strangers, but she had a sweet, clear soprano that blended with her sister's. Together, they sang their way through "Ain't Misbehavin'." They giggled at the risqué lyrics to Eddie Cantor's "Makin' Whoopie." With each song, Gladys felt Bunny warming up, being more herself.

Then Bunny stood up, as if something suddenly occurred to her. She wandered into the living room, looking around at the chairs, the wall hangings, and the curtains, as if she had stumbled into a stranger's house. Gladys watched her with peripheral vision while she flipped through the sheet music.

I'll get by

As long as I have you.

Bunny sat on the couch. Gladys paused.

"¿Tienes hambre?"

Bunny shook her head and looked down. Gladys stood and crossed over to her.

"No!" Bunny protested. "Keep playing!"

"I'm tired."

Bunny went to the radio and turned it on. Tuning through the stations, she found some dance music and smiled.

"¡Vamos a bailar!" she sang.

Gladys sighed and smiled. She rose and put her arms around her sister, and they fox-trotted around the room while a crooner sang from the radio.

Every star above knows the one I love

Sweet Sue, just you.

Inside music, almost any music, Gladys felt safe. It was a country where she spoke the language and was listened to. And now, with her sister in her arms, she closed her eyes and felt the notes swirling around them, holding them in a place where sadness could be stilled. If she could keep Bunny here, everything would be all right. But when she looked into Bunny's face, she saw that her eyes were welling with tears.

"¿Que pasó?" Gladys whispered.

Headlights flashed across the window as they heard the gravel crunch of Jack's car pulling into the driveway. Bunny looked startled; she stepped back, sniffled, and quickly wiped her eyes. Gladys combed her hair back with her fingers.

"Hizzoner is home!" Gladys said.

Bunny's lips trembled into a smile. When the door opened, she rushed to Jack and put her arms around him. He dropped his briefcase and embraced her. She kissed him deeply on the lips and then a dozen times on his face. Taking his hand, she pulled him into the living room.

"Glad and I were dancing. Come, let's dance!"

Jack smiled, resisted briefly, and then took off his hat and jacket and followed her into the room. Putting his hand firmly around her waist, he spun her into a dance.

"How was your day, my darling?" Bunny asked theatrically.

"Horrible!" he said brightly. "The world is going to hell!"

"Oh, rotten luck!"

"And what did you do today, Bunny darling?"

"I cried and cried!"

"You must be exhausted!"

"Not at all!"

He twirled her.

Gladys fell onto the couch. Thank God, Jack was home. She watched them as they danced for two numbers. It was nearly eleven, and she rose to say good night.

"No!" Bunny cried, turning to Gladys. "You and Jack dance. I'll make drinks." Jack and Gladys looked at each other shyly. "Come on, you two!"

"Darling, it's very late," said Jack. "Maybe we should all . . ."

"Nonsense. Let's have a nightcap. I want to see some dancing!"

Jack held his hand out for Gladys, who took it and stepped toward him. Bunny smiled and hurried to the kitchen. For a moment, Jack and Gladys danced for Bunny's benefit but stopped when she was out of the room. They searched each other's eyes for a moment and then turned away. They were each, in their own way, experts on Bunny—together, they knew her better than anybody in the world. But at moments like these, neither knew what to do. And in waiting for the other to take charge, they floundered together.

"How long has she . . .?" he began.

They could hear ice clinking into glasses. "Will the mayor like a Scotch?" Bunny called out.

"Yes, thank you," he called back.

"And Gladys Verga of the concert stage, what will you be drinking this evening? A Bee's Knees?"

"Scotch."

"Keeping it simple for the bartender. Much appreciated." Bunny brought the drinks on a small tray. "Don't forget to tip your server," she said.

Jack and Gladys sat across from each other and sipped their drinks. The Scotch was sharp and unpleasant. Bunny swayed around the room to the music. She took a sip from her glass and grimaced. "Oh, Jack! Will you convene the village council and repeal the Volstead Act so we can get some decent hooch around here?"

"Yes, of course. Any other constitutional amendments you would like to get rid of?"

"Too much bother. Maybe just secede from the union."

"To the Republic of Plandome!" Jack raised his glass.

"For life, liberty, and drinkable Scotch!" Bunny laughed. The radio orchestra's crescendo was met by applause. Bunny bowed and then frowned at them. "The two of you! You should have married each other and sent me back to Waterloo with Mama."

"Darling, what a thing to say," Jack said.

"It's true! You would have had the perfect wife for your perfect home, who would have thrown fabulous parties. And Glad could still give concerts.

And give you babies. And happiness." Bunny smiled. "You would both be happy, I know it. I know it. Why did you ever marry me?"

"Because I love you," Jack said.

Gladys stood up, crossed the room, and turned off the radio. "Jack loves you. I love you. Enough of this. It's time for bed."

Bunny grabbed onto Gladys's arms. *"¡Lo siento! ¡Lo siento mucho!"*

"No te preocupes. Vamos a la cama."

Jack rose and took Bunny's hand. "Gladys is right, darling. It's time."

"No! No!" Bunny cried, turning away from them both.

"Then tell us what's wrong!" Jack cried. "We can't help you unless you tell us."

"Soy lo que está mal."

Jack looked at Gladys. "What does that mean?"

Gladys watched her sister and understood. Bunny knew she was sick, just as Emmah knew she was sick. She knew the burden she had put on everyone around her. But, while their mother wanted nothing more than to hold them close, fearful of the world, Bunny hated the thought of trapping people she loved. She was what was wrong.

Jack finally shook his head and walked to the kitchen. "I'm calling Dr. Evers."

"What good will that do?" Gladys snapped. Bunny looked at Gladys, her eyes pleading.

"Jack!" Gladys called out as she followed him.

"I'm not doing this again. She needs a doctor's care!"

Gladys drew close and whispered sharply, "She's been under a doctor's care for over a year and look at her. He will just drug her to sleep."

"Maybe that's what she needs," he shot back.

"She needs you."

Jack picked up the phone receiver. "She has me."

Gladys walked back to find Bunny on the couch, tears streaming down her cheeks, as she heard Jack make the call, waking the doctor. She looked up. Gladys took Bunny's hand and led her up the stairs and into the bedroom. She helped her change into her nightgown and get into bed. Climbing in beside her, Gladys held and rocked her sister, who began to heave and sob.

It was after one in the morning when Dr. Evers arrived. He had short white hair and thin wire glasses and was, as usual, nattily dressed in suit and dark bow tie. He carried a black bag. Having attended to Bunny many times over the past year, he was familiar with the house and went straight to the bedroom. Jack followed him in.

"Bunny, darling. Tell me what's wrong," Evers said. Bunny shook her head and turned away. He set down his bag and took off his hat. "Gladys, please bring us a glass of water."

"No, no, no, no!" Bunny cried.

"It's OK, darling," Jack said.

"Let me take a look at you."

Gladys rose and went downstairs to fetch the water, which meant he was going to give her a sleeping powder. *Let her rest. All will be well in the morning.* It was the same routine over and over. When she returned with the glass of water, Evers was talking quietly to Bunny, who seemed to have calmed down. He took a small box from his bag and opened a packet of powder and poured it into the water.

"Jack, Gladys. Why don't you both take a break? I'll stay here until she's relaxed."

Gladys and Jack sat across from each other in the living room, exhausted. Evers stayed upstairs for close to an hour. They could hear his calming voice but very little from Bunny, which was a relief. The house was quiet again, and they could breathe.

They heard the bedroom door open and shut. Evers walked down the stairs, carrying his bag, wearing an expression of tired satisfaction. He reached the bottom landing and, turning to them, opened his mouth to speak, when a shot rang out.

Gladys froze. Jack was the first up the stairs. He let out a cry of horror in a voice she had never heard. Gladys and the doctor ran up to find Jack cradling Bunny on the floor of the bedroom. Blood poured from her chest, and her eyes were wide open with terror. On the floor beside her was a black revolver.

"Bunny! Bunny! Oh, God!"

Evers fell to his knees and put his hand on the wound. Blood flowed through his fingers. Gladys stood in the doorway and watched her sister die.

When Gladys woke up on Saturday, the feeling of loss was a physical pain that stung her whole body, rendering it nearly immobile. She lay in bed as the room slowly brightened. There was nothing to do. Turning her face back into her pillow, she felt, not for the first time, the sweet pull of darkness that had swallowed her mother and sister. She thought of Bunny's eyes, so filled with pain and fear as she lay bleeding, slowly soften and relax as she passed away right before her. When the world emptied off her. Was it worth it—to step through that violent portal to finally be at peace? Was it peace? A wave of pain stung her, and Gladys could feel her eyes fill with tears. This was the cost of Bunny's release. This debt of anguish passed on to the living.

Gladys heard the soft slap of a newspaper landing on their porch. She felt the instinct to rise and see what Hal had written. But then it drained out. What did it matter what the goddamned *Great Neck News* published about Bunny? She was gone. Who will remember her beautiful smile and loving nature? We will all be forgotten. Gladys had sung and acted before hundreds of thousands of people all over the country for over a decade. What did she have to show for it? Who would remember her? And when the last person who remembers you dies, are you even alive? Are you even dead? If she joined her sister and mother today, would the world even notice? Who would pick up the legacy of pain and carry it forward?

The front door opened and closed downstairs. Jack was home. He had been dealing with the police, the coroner, and, presumably, the undertaker. There was a funeral to plan. She needed to try again to reach Artie. Maybe Ruth could help.

On the dining room table, Gladys found a pile of opened cards and telegrams and a folded *Daily News* with the headline:

L.I. MAYOR'S WIFE PUTS BULLET IN HEART

She quickly turned the paper over to hide the article. Next to that was the glossy *Great Neck News.* She opened it. Wedged between wedding announcements and society bulletins was a narrow column.

BUNNY OLNEY
By Hal W. Lanigan

> *As dear and as lovely a little woman as ever lived was Mrs. Jack Olney of Plandome Road, Plandome, whose death last Thursday stunned her many friends.*

She scanned down the article:

> *... sweet little soul ... everything to live for ... her sister Gladys Verga of the concert stage ... no more delightful little lady ... always full of life and as wholesome as she was sweet ... when we heard of her death ... we could scarcely believe it. ...*

And then at the bottom:

Jack Olney, man among men, knows well how his myriad of friends feel. His loss is unmendable. God never took to his bosom a finer, sweeter little soul than Bunny. She was kindness itself, charitable to a lasting degree.

Good for you, Hal, she thought. *You didn't screw it up.*

THE GURU HAD
AN OFF NIGHT

The eyes of the acolytes brimmed with warmth as we stepped out of the elevator to the dizzying views of the 102nd floor of the shiny new One World Trade Center.

"Welcome!" beamed a white woman in a pale-yellow sari as she took my hand. "I'm so pleased you could come!"

I gripped her hand to steady myself as my eyes adjusted to the disorienting sight of New York Harbor far below. I thanked her and introduced my son.

"Hello, Henry!" she marveled, taking his hand. He switched instantly from his practiced cynicism ("A guru, Dad? Really?") into the charming nineteen-year-old, accustomed to talking to adults. He pushed his long black hair back from his face and smiled.

The waiters pressed forward with mango mocktails, and we took in the large space with floor-to-ceiling windows high above the earth. The Statue of Liberty was a small dot below. Jersey to the right, Brooklyn, left. The room—bright, empty, and open—was filling with guests who had come, like us, to hear Gurudev Shankara speak. I spotted Dev, the man who invited us, talking and laughing with a small group. He was an Indian American and had, like his friends, the patina of wealth about him: the cut of his suit, his hair, his glasses, his confidence. I hovered for a moment and then approached him. He, too, was delighted to see me and introduced us to his friends: smiles, smiles, welcomes.

"Gurudev has absolutely changed my life," Dev declared. "But I've never been in his *presence* before," he added excitedly. "Henry, do you meditate?"

Henry shook his head.

"Oh, you have to learn. The Gurudev has breathing techniques that cure you of stress."

I watched my son talk to Dev. I liked watching him. He was becoming a man before my eyes. It warmed me and sometimes unsettled me. I was more comfortable as the father of a little boy than of a teenager, even less so now of a young man. I knew his adolescent retreat from me—his privacy and his pushing back—were signs of successful parenting. But I wondered, always, if I had done my job. Did my own need for privacy, my own pulling away, damage or deny him what he needed from me? It didn't look that way. He turned from Dev toward me, and I caught in his eye a wink of irony: *What a joke!*

He was here and he wasn't here. I wanted to be here. I wanted us both to be. Why? I didn't know Dev well and his invitation came as a total surprise. I thought, *Why not meet an authentic Indian guru? What if this was an open door for a midlife spiritual journey, a space between religion and wellness for this atheist?* I had never been in the presence of a holy man before either. I was curious and ready. Henry was hungry and attacked a small buffet of precious vegetarian dishes in bamboo steamers.

"John! I'm so glad you are here!" said a woman in a long blue robe. "The work you do is so important!"

I shook her hand and smiled, realizing that I had been Googled. It was both surprising and mildly exhilarating. Being important. Being recognized for good works. Maybe I belonged here among the rich and elevated. She said her name quickly, and I immediately forgot it. I tried to read her nametag, which was partially covered in the folds of her cloth. Her life had also been changed by Gurudev. "I worked in capital markets for years. I was miserable," she told me. "Now I run a chocolate factory in New Jersey."

"How did your family feel about your change of career?"

"They didn't like it," she smiled, adding something about immigrant parents and their expectations, their insistence on security above all other concerns.

As we talked, she kept her eyes brightly focused on me, as if I was the only person in the room. That was her gift. I liked it. It made me feel welcomed and ready to be open and honest myself. And that was the general vibe of the fifty-or-so guests who mingled and shined on one another. They were mostly middle-aged and about half were southeast Asian. I saw one tall, bald Black man in an expensive leather jacket, standing aloof, surveying the crowd. The sun was setting brightly and the reddening light forgave all our blemishes, making us all sparkle warmly in giddy anticipation of enlightenment.

I'd seen faces like these before. I've worn one of those faces. But that was different. And a long time ago. At least here, no one was selling anything. There was no enrollment. It felt pure.

The mocktail was undrinkable. I put it down and weaved through the room. I found Henry talking to a long-haired man in a scarf. "I used to work in tech," the man was explaining. "Now I run a startup called Tushy. We're bringing back bidets."

"What's a bidet?" asked Henry.

He was better at this than I was. Or better at faking it. Really, he was better than me at his age in so many ways. Like the time in high school when he broke up with a girl because *it didn't feel healthy*. He didn't have sex with her because *he wasn't ready*. I didn't even have that language at sixteen, much less the self-esteem—or self-restraint—to act on it. There were so many ways I admired my son, but I rarely found the words or the time to say them to him. When he was little, I knew everything about him. But as he grew, I knew less and less. I found myself watching, looking for clues, begging for scraps. He could tell, so he withheld.

The signal was given for guests to move to the presentation area—fifty cushioned chairs arching in rows around a small platform with a couch and microphone. Henry and I found seats, midway down, hugging the aisle.

I hadn't expected to be reminded of The Sterling Institute of Relationship, to which I gave five years of my late twenties in what began as a desperate search for answers to why my relationships with women had been so painful and brief. Justin Sterling, the swaggering guru of what I discovered was a cult sometime after I'd joined, had simple, punchy answers, which all boiled down to: *It was the women's fault*. The solution was to spend more time with men. Join a men's team. "Embrace all men" was the mantra. For a time, it worked. I made friends and found a circle of acceptance. It was the initiation that I had never had. I rose in leadership. But it was bullshit. When I was eventually kicked out for apostasy, all those friends vanished. Decades later, I wondered how I could have surrendered myself to it. But I knew why. Being here, on top of the world, surrounded by nice people who leaned forward in their chairs as the sun set, I could feel the attraction again, the pull of promise: *There is an answer. This man has it.*

Henry sat beside me, his eyes down on his phone, with hair again covering his face. "What do you think?" I asked.

"Everybody here is *rich*," he muttered in disgust.

"Except us," I corrected.

There was a stir and a craning of necks as a small, brown, bearded man in white robes walked smiling into the room and took the stage. Across the room, a smattering of applause began uncertainly until it was picked up by the rest of us, and soon, we were standing and clapping as the Gurudev stepped up on the platform, nodding in gratitude. Rather than sitting, he adjusted the mic stand. The room quietened quickly as we all sat and grinned.

"Thank you," Gurudev said. "What a beautiful sunset!"

All heads swiveled right, as if we hadn't noticed the red ball over Jersey.

"What a beautiful room. I am so pleased to be here in New York City." He paused, as if to gather his thoughts. "I was thinking on the way here about dispassion. It is a very difficult time. We are very divided. There is a lot of passion. Everybody is passionate. Angry. Who is dispassionate? Meditation helps us nurture dispassion, right?"

People nodded in assent.

"Depression is having no passion. No aggression. So, is passion bad?"

He let his question hang in the air unanswered. He then adjusted the microphone. We stared at him. He smiled at us. He began to talk about his work as a peacemaker around the world. He claimed to have mediated conflicts in Kashmir and to have convinced Columbian guerillas to lay down their arms, all through the power of meditation. I could see my history-loving son's eyebrows rise. It was all a little hard to follow . . . a kind of humble bragging on steroids sprinkled with aphorisms ("Worldly love is like an ocean; it has a bottom. Divine love is like the sky . . ."), presented offhand, as statements of the obvious. It was spirituality that did not require much sacrifice. "Austerity comes out of abundance and brings abundance."

It was OK to be rich.

And still, I must admit, I bent forward along with the rest. I suspended disbelief. However, I couldn't help but compare this holy man's meandering presentation with the guru of my youth. Justin Sterling didn't fuck around. "We live in a dangerously feminized society," he announced to cheers as he entered the hall, crowded with men. I was twenty-seven. His philosophy was black and white. "Women are primarily driven by relationships. Men are primarily driven by competition. Women express feelings through words. Men express feelings through action. Relationships for men are enemy, hostile territory. Women are one hundred percent responsible for relationships." Zinger after zinger. "The badder the boy, the better the man!" Cue the cheers and hoots. I leaned in then as well—so desperate was I for answers to why I couldn't fall or stay in love. Within twenty-four hours of that Men's Weekend, sleep-deprived and hungry, I was squeezed into a clutch of sweaty men, grieving for my father, with tears dropping down my cheeks in a kind of mass empathy for the pain in all men everywhere. I was no longer separate and apart—I was accepted and transformed. It was astonishing.

I looked at my son next to me, the face of dispassion. Never in a million years would he fall for Justin's crap. He clearly had no use for Gurudev's gentle maxims either. He held fast to his discernment and intellectual distance. *There's a fortress around him,* I thought.

"Do we want to meditate?" Gurudev asked brightly to happy murmurs of approval. "Breathing is the doorway to healing, yes?"

Arms were dropped to laps, backs straightened, and bottoms adjusted, as everyone closed their eyes through the guided exercise.

"Raise your hands above your head and shake them," said Gurudev.

I snuck a peak. It was quite a sight: fifty well-dressed people shaking their arms and hands spastically with eyes closed. All except Henry.

Soon, we were all still and breathing together, and the room became silent. I tried, vainly, to clear my mind of thoughts. I focused on the shifting fields of red and orange inside my eyelids. I counted my breaths. I lost count and tried again. I felt Henry beside me. "A father's job is to prepare his son for the world," Justin said. "Don't worry about being a good father, worry about making a good son." *Easy for him to say,* I thought. Did my father ever think in those terms? I ended up in Justin's cult because I did not feel prepared for the world. Was I a better father because I watched my son and worried?

The meditation ended, and Gurudev opened the floor for questions. The sun had set, and the windows around us were alive with the glittering nightscape high above the city.

"I know many successful people," said a man in a blue suit, "but why are people with everything still unhappy?"

"Because they think spirituality is incompatible with business," replied Gurudev. "Spirituality brings ethics to business."

"How do you balance materialism with spirituality?" a woman asked.

"How can one exist without the other? If you are hungry, you cannot take comfort in spirituality. The mind–body complex needs both material comfort and spiritual comfort."

The one Black man in the room raised his hand and was called on. He stood up and introduced himself. He was from Haiti and was disgusted by the government there. "Why is it that when politicians gain power, they lose touch with the people and become despots?"

Gurudev smiled. He talked again about his work in Kashmir and Columbia. "When I speak to leaders, I ask them how they want to be seen by history," he said.

"But what if they don't care about history? What if they are greedy and corrupt?"

"When I talk to them one-on-one, when I ask them to meditate with me, I find, they do care."

"But what can I do for my country? I cannot go to the palace in Port-au-Prince and ask the president to meditate with me. My people are being crushed."

Gurudev smiled again . . .

Asking questions of Justin Sterling was not for the faint-hearted. I remembered attending a reunion event with Justin and a hundred or more

Sterling leaders. I was probably four years in and was losing patience with the whole organization. I had met Stephanie—my future wife and Henry's future mom—who called me out on the misogyny I had internalized. Justin's zingers weren't working in real life.

"How do I know if I'm ready to get married?" I asked Justin, who sat in a tall director's chair on the stage above us.

"She's putting pressure on you, right?"

There were murmurs and chuckles among the men seated around me. I smiled.

"Of course, she is," he continued. "Is the relationship one hundred percent on your terms?"

"I'm struggling with that. I'm not sure how a relationship can be on one person's terms."

"Sounds like you're struggling a lot. Why do you want to get married?"

"I love her." Laughter.

"Men marry for love. Women marry for security. Can you support her?"

"Not by myself."

"Do you want children with her?"

"Someday, maybe."

"Listen to yourself. Maybe. Maybe. Terms? What terms? I bet she's your best friend, right?" More laughter, rich with pity. "Right?"

I looked at him.

"Only get married when you are completely self-sufficient. Never need a woman for anything. She's not your friend. She wants to change you. The moment she does, she'll lose interest. Because you don't know who you are." He turned to the audience.

"Is this man ready for marriage?"

"NO!" came the resounding shout.

He turned to me. "Do this poor woman a favor—let her go. She needs a real man. You're not ready. Trust me. Trust the men."

I came back home that night and broke Stephanie's heart. I woke up in the middle of the night and heard her sobbing in the next room. The Sterling Institute of Relationship was destroying the only relationship that mattered to me. I had no idea what to do. Why Stephanie didn't leave me then, why she stuck with me, and why she believed in me, I never really understood. But it was she who ultimately initiated me into manhood, husband-hood, and fatherhood.

I looked again at my beautiful, mysterious son. I wondered if I would ever really see him for who he was, the way Stephanie saw me, beneath my fortress of beliefs and deflections. Would Henry ever see me as anything other than his father? *We're mysteries to each other*, I thought, *filling out expectations to meet and miss*. But one thing was for sure: if I had listened to my guru, Henry wouldn't be here.

Gurudev finished his talk to a thunderous applause. Henry turned to me. "Can we get out of here?"

"In a minute," I said.

I found Dev standing at the back and watching, while people crowded around Gurudev to take selfies. I thanked him for inviting us. He looked disappointed. "He's usually better than this," he said, shaking his head. "He connects the dots better."

I shrugged. "Even holy men have an off night now and then."

He smiled, embarrassed, and shook my hand. "He really changed my life," he assured me.

I found Henry, who had been handed a colorful flyer advertising classes and workshops we could take to learn Gurudev's teachings and techniques.

"Here. We can learn to meditate for a thousand dollars," he grinned. It was an enrollment event after all.

On the way out, Henry and I stopped by one of the huge windows to take in the view one last time. From a hundred stories in the air, New York's cityscape was a reverse Milky Way, the sky blue-black above a million tiny lights sparkling to the horizon. As Henry pressed his phone against the glass to take a picture, the angled windows mirrored us back as shadowy forms: father and son floating, faceless, above the sunken stars.

ACKNOWLEDGMENTS

My deepest gratitude to everyone who read, responded to, and helped nurture these stories-in-progress. Thanks to Rob, Stacia and Kermit for their early encouragement and thoughtful questions. Thanks to Pam, for the inspiration and the permission to write about Uncle Duck. Many thanks to the Post-Sackett Writing Group: Tim, Signe, Helena, Anastasia, Sheryl and Maame for the weekly discipline and essential guidance from writers I respect and admire. Thanks to Susan and Peter for giving me space and inspiration to write while surrounded by genius. Special thanks to my editor, Walter Bode. And always, and ever, thanks to Stephanie and Henry.

WHO THE HECK IS...?

John Collins Williams is an award-winning producer and film-maker and co-founder of Reel Works, a nonprofit in Brooklyn. He lives in Long Island with his wife, son, corgi, mutt, and cats. This is his first collection of short stories.